D1575530

The Treasure of the Orkins

A Magical World Awaits You

Read

and coming soon

THE SECRETS OF DROON

— TONY ABBOTT —

The Treasure of the Orkins

Illustrated by Royce Fitzgerald

Cover illustration by Tim Jessell

SCHOLASTIC INC.
New York Toronto London Auckland Sydney
Mexico City New Delhi Hong Kong Buenos Aires

To my family,
the real treasure

For more information about the continuing saga of Droon,
please visit Tony Abbott's website at
www.tonyabbottbooks.com

No part of this publication may be reproduced, stored in a
retrieval system, or transmitted in any form or by any means,
electronic, mechanical, photocopying, recording, or otherwise,
without written permission of the publisher.
For information regarding permission, write to Scholastic Inc.,
Attention: Permissions Department, 557 Broadway, New York, NY 10012.

ISBN-13: 978-0-439-90253-3
ISBN-10: 0-439-90253-3

Text copyright © 2008 by Tony Abbott.
Illustrations copyright © 2008 by Scholastic Inc.

All rights reserved. Published by Scholastic Inc.
SCHOLASTIC, LITTLE APPLE, and associated logos
are trademarks and/or registered trademarks of Scholastic Inc.

12 11 10 9 8 7 6 5 4 3   9 10 11 12 13/0

Contents

One

Out of the Blue

"Hurry up for breakfast, dear!"

Eric Hinkle didn't answer his mother's call. He was in bed, fast asleep and dreaming.

In his dream, a blinding snowstorm whirled all around him. It showered him with icy cold snowflakes.

Icy cold *blue* snowflakes!

"Waffles!" called his father.

Eric didn't hear him, either. "This must be Droon," he said to himself as he watched the flakes fly over his head. "Where else would I see blue snow?"

Droon was the magical world that he and his friends Neal and Julie had discovered one day under his basement stairs.

It was a land of strange and fabulous places and people, a world of adventure and mystery, and it was the *only* place where the snow would ever be bright blue!

Whooosh! Sudden gusts of wind magically spun the snowflakes around Eric's head into a crown of glittering blue.

"How cool!" he said, his breath becoming visible, then fading in the frosty air.

As a magical world, Droon was full of strange secrets and odd mysteries.

What had happened to the once-evil sorcerer called Lord Sparr?

Did the word *Reki-ur-set,* which the sorceress Salamandra had told him again and again, mean something special to him or was it just nonsense?

Was the moon dragon Gethwing alive, or had he perished in Droon's Underworld?

And perhaps most important of all, what did the future hold for him and his friends?

Strangely, Eric loved the mystery of these questions. He almost didn't want them to be answered. Once they *were* answered, he thought, the magic of Droon might come to an end. And that was something he couldn't bear to think about.

Ever since he had developed his own powers, magic had become a part of Eric's life that he never wanted to go away.

His friends had developed magical abilities since then, too. Neal had become a genie, and Julie could fly like a bird.

Eric sometimes felt that together, the friends' powers were nearly as strong as those of the old master wizard, Galen Longbeard.

Wait . . . Galen? Galen!

As Eric peered through the whooshing snow of his dream, he thought he saw the great wizard himself, trekking slowly through the deep blue drifts.

Eric took a step. "Galen? Is that you?"

The figure stopped and turned. It *was* Galen. His face was pale, his long white beard blown wildly by the wind.

He fixed Eric with his eyes.

He opened his lips to speak.

"Eric, hurry. Hurry —"

Eric jumped from his bed, completely awake. "Galen?"

"— or I'm going to eat your breakfast for you!" his father called up from the kitchen.

Eric blinked awake, then laughed. "Whoa! My dad's words in Galen's mouth. It's like Galen called me himself! And blue snow? We're totally being called to Droon. I need to get dressed right away —" He hurried to his closet door and pulled it wide open . . .

. . . only to see the face of his friend Neal, hanging upside down from the ceiling.

"Did somebody say 'waffles'?" Neal asked.

"Ahhhhhh!" Eric screamed.

"*Shhh!*" hissed Julie, whose face bobbed down right next to Neal's. "Don't let your parents hear you!"

Eric staggered back. "You guys scared me! What are you doing up there?"

"I floated through the attic window," said Neal, pointing up. "Did you know that there's a trapdoor in your closet ceiling?"

Eric looked up. Sure enough, there was a door there. "No, I didn't know that. Listen, we have to go to Droon. I just had a dream about blue snowflakes. Galen called me, sort of. There's a new adventure waiting for us."

"Cool," said Neal. "I'm so ready to be a genie again."

"Wait," said Julie. "It's Saturday. Don't your parents have chores for you to do?"

Eric groaned. "I forgot about chores."

"So let's float back outside and then sneak in your basement window," said Neal.

Eric shook his head. "My mom and dad are waiting for me. But I have an idea. You guys come over and pretend to surprise me. If you really beg me to hang out, maybe I can get out of doing my chores for a while."

Julie smiled. "Sounds like a plan. But first, take that oversized blueberry off your head, Neal. People will talk."

Neal pulled his genie turban off, folded it into a bite-size shape, and slid it into his pocket. "Don't be scared. I'm just me again."

Julie laughed. "Now I'm really scared!"

After checking to make sure that no one could see them, Neal and Julie linked hands and drifted through the attic window and down to the ground. Eric quickly washed and dressed, then ran into the kitchen.

He plopped down at the table with his parents and waited anxiously for Neal and Julie to come to the door.

"One more minute and that waffle would have been mine!" his father said as he set a plate in front of him. "Besides, you'll need your strength. It's chore day, after all."

Eric frowned. "Thanks. Did you hear anyone at the back door?"

"I don't think so," said his mother. "But speaking of chores, you won't believe what I found in the basement."

Eric grew nervous. "The basement? What did you find in the basement?"

Mrs. Hinkle set an old photograph by his plate. It was a picture of a middle-aged man standing by a large white building. Eric pretended to be interested, but all he could think about was getting to Droon.

"Do you know who this is?" she asked.

Eric shook his head. "No. Hey, did any-one hear a knock?"

"It's my grandfather's grandfather," Mrs. Hinkle went on. "He flew a racing plane. It had funny curved wings and was painted blue. He won a lot of races in his day."

Eric remembered hearing about him. He had once done research on his great-great-great-grandfather for a school project. He *was* interested. He really was. But Galen had called him to Droon. Wasn't that more important right now? "Uh-huh . . . that's neat. . . ."

Using silent words, he called to his friends. ***Neal! Julie! Where are you guys?***

Knock! Knock!

Eric jumped up and tore open the back door. "Oh! Neal and Julie!" he said. "What a surprise to see you here!"

"ERIC!" Neal practically shouted. "Can you hang out? PLEEEEEEASE?"

"Oh, I'd love to!" said Eric, turning toward his parents. "But I have chores to do."

He nudged Julie secretly.

Julie smiled sweetly at Mr. and Mrs. Hinkle. "Is it all right if the three of us go to the basement for a little while?" She smiled again.

There was a pause as Eric's parents stared at the three friends.

"Actually," said Mrs. Hinkle, "I *want* you to go downstairs. That's where Eric's chore is. It's finally time to clean the basement!"

"Clean the basement?" repeated Neal. "This is like *déjà vu* all over again!"

The three friends remembered that their first visit to Droon began when they were supposed to be cleaning the basement.

"But, Mom —" Eric started.

"No buts," said Mrs. Hinkle. "Your father promised to remodel the basement a long time ago. And he's decided to start today!"

Mr. Hinkle looked up from his newspaper, chewing his last piece of waffle. "I habbb?"

"You have," said Mrs. Hinkle. "It's time that we built a proper playroom down there."

Mr. Hinkle swallowed his waffle. "You know, you're right. I'll start this morning, or maybe just after lunch. This week, for sure —"

"Today is part of this week," said Mrs. Hinkle, smiling. "I'll get your work gloves."

As his parents began to get things ready, Eric took his friends downstairs. "This is the worst! What are we going to do?"

"I've been afraid of this since the beginning," said Julie. "If the basement is remodeled, the magical staircase in the closet will be revealed. And Droon won't be a secret anymore! We have to think of a way to stall your dad."

Neal whipped out his turban and planted it on his head. "Thanks to my thinking cap, I already have an idea."

Eric looked at him. "What?"

"Let's say we do 'help' your dad," said Neal. "But we do such a bad job helping that we get nowhere. With all of us doing our worst, it will take forever!"

Julie smiled. "That just might work! Let's think it over in Droon. Since no time passes here once we're down there, we'll work out the details in a flash."

"Good idea, guys," said Eric. "Let's move."

The three friends piled into the small closet under the basement stairs. Eric switched off the light and — *whoosh!* —

the floor became the top step of a stairway leading through a bright pink sky to the world of Droon.

But as soon as the kids started down the stairs, winds buffeted them this way and that. Clouds barreled out of nowhere and thickened the air around them. They heard blasts of thunder and the crackle of lightning.

"A storm!" cried Julie. "Hold on tight —"

Rooooarrrr! A terrifying noise filled the air.

Before the children could move, a huge shape with fluttering wings dived from the clouds with amazing speed — and charged right at them!

Two

North of Jaffa

Roooaaarrrr!

The dark-winged creature swept so close that Julie lost her footing. "Whoa! Help —"

"Got you!" said Neal, grabbing her arm and pulling her safely back to the staircase.

Eric tried to steady himself, but his fingers sparked suddenly and — *blam!* — he shot a blast of silver sparks at the shrouded shape.

At the same moment, a gust of wind cleared the sky. The dark creature revealed itself as none other than Keeah's four-winged, long-bodied flying ship, the *Dragonfly*!

Eric's blast sizzled across the air toward it.

"No, no!" he said. "Please go wild!"

His shot was not wild. But just as it reached the plane, the *Dragonfly*'s nose popped open and — *slurrrk!* — the entire blast was swallowed up inside. The ship jumped and bumped, it wobbled and bobbled, then righted, slowed, and hovered mere inches from the rainbow stairs.

Pop! The cockpit dome sprang open and out peered the green-haired head of Friddle, the airship's inventor. "Welcome, old friends!"

"I'm so sorry!" said Eric hurriedly. "My sparks have a mind of their own sometimes."

"Not to worry," the inventor said over the sound of the sputtering engine. "I'm just happy my new antiblast system works. Come. You are wanted!"

No sooner had the three children climbed into the plane than Friddle turned to a seat beside him. "Are you ready, copilot?"

"Aye-aye!" chirped the familiar voice of Max the spider troll, who turned to wave at the friends. Then, pushing one lever after another, Max banked the *Dragonfly* smoothly away from the steps and began to steer it toward the ground.

Eric saw that snow was beginning to powder the fields below. He realized at once that this was like his dream, only the snowflakes here were normal and white.

"Landing!" Max chirped. He flipped a red switch, and two giant snow skis slid down from under the wings and popped into place. The *Dragonfly* dipped, bumped, and then slid across the snowy ground to a stop.

Within moments, two riders galloped toward the plane. Galen, in his tall hat and midnight-blue cloak, rode his shaggy pilka, Leep. Queen Relna, dressed head to foot in snow-dappled furs, raced by his side. Together their pilkas' twelve hooves sprayed wild plumes of snow behind them.

"Our passengers have arrived!" said Galen, jumping to the ground and striding quickly to the ship.

"After testing the *Dragonfly*'s latest improvement," said Friddle, "we're ready for anything and everything!"

"Which we shall undoubtedly encounter," added the wizard, "once Keeah joins us."

"Are we going on a journey?" asked Julie, when the children climbed from the plane.

"To the land of constant snows," said Relna. "Beyond the Ice Hills of Tarabat."

"I dreamed about snow," said Eric, looking from the queen to the wizard. "Blue snow. Maybe we'll see some on this adventure."

Galen's brow wrinkled in thought. "Blue snow. The legend speaks of blue snowflakes."

"Really?" said Eric. "There's a legend?"

The queen nodded. "One hundred years ago exactly, a great storm ravaged the far north of Droon. It is said that snow — blue snow — fell from the sky like jewels."

"Perhaps more important," said Galen, "the storm caused a rift between our two worlds, allowing anyone to pass between them."

Neal gasped. "Even bad guys?"

The wizard nodded. "Even them. A storm just like that one has formed in the north. It is our duty to guard the passage between the worlds to make sure it remains unused."

"Where's Keeah?" asked Julie.

Relna smiled. "Keeah has gone to Lumpland to recruit a special friend."

"Khan, king of the Lumpies," added Max. "He's perfect on an adventure!"

The children all remembered the noble, pillow-shaped ruler of the Lumpy clan. Besides being a good friend, Khan was a gifted traveler. His ability to sniff out danger made him a big help on any mission.

"I didn't exactly dress for snow," said Neal, shivering under his turban. "Genies are desert folk, mostly."

"No matter," said the spider troll. "We have a full wardrobe of winter gear!"

No sooner had he showed them a compartment on the plane that was filled with furs, boots, hoods, and gloves than Relna called out, "And look! Our journey begins."

The children could just make out their friend Keeah, racing across the plains on a pilka. Her long blond hair flowed in the wind behind her. She galloped up and leaped to the ground breathlessly.

"We can't go north!" she exclaimed. "Lumpland is completely surrounded by a sandstorm. My father and I couldn't get

through it. He sent me to bring rein-forcements."

The children all looked to Galen.

"We cannot wait, either," the wizard said. "Our window of time is closing as we speak. Soon, the passage will be open. Evil elements may enter your world . . . or discover ours. It's very dangerous. Relna, what do you say?"

"We must undertake both journeys," the queen said. "Galen, I will come with you to the north."

"And I will go with the children to Lumpland," said Max.

The wizard nodded. "So, two journeys instead of one. All the more reason to use these." He pulled a pair of saddlebags from his pilka. When he set them on the ground, the packs jumped, fell over, and wiggled as if whatever was inside wanted to get out.

Neal stepped back and wrinkled his nose. "Squirrels?"

"No, no," said Galen with a chuckle. He carefully opened both packs. "Old friends."

He removed two balls, one red, one blue. Both were glowing as if they were alive.

"The magical spheres of Doobesh," said Galen. "The Ruby Orb and the Sapphire Star."

"I don't like that red one," said Max, sidling away from the Ruby Orb. "It was very cramped in there."

Everyone remembered how the Ruby Orb of Doobesh had once imprisoned Max inside it and had flown him halfway across the world.

"I have tamed them," said Galen, handing the Ruby Orb to Eric and giving him a small pouch to carry it in. "Since the twin spheres seek each other, they will help us stay connected on separate journeys. We go today to the snowy north, you to the sandy south."

Eric's heart thumped in his chest. If he was going south with Keeah, then why had he dreamed about blue snowflakes? If they were part of a legend, why wasn't he going north, where he might see them?

Were his dreams playing tricks on him?

Vroooom-pop-pop! The clattering of the *Dragonfly*'s engine set the two groups in motion. The wizard and the queen joined Friddle in the cockpit of the plane, while the children and Max climbed onto their pilkas.

"Everyone ready?" Galen asked, holding his hand up. When the children nodded, he lowered his hand quickly. "Let's be off!" he cried.

With a great roar, the four-winged *Dragonfly* lifted and skimmed over the ground, picking up speed by the second.

On the fields below, the pilkas nosed one another, and Keeah, Eric, Neal, Julie, and Max galloped off to the sunny, snowless southern lands.

Three

The Magic Pyramid

Mile after mile, the five friends rode — past royal Jaffa City, beyond the Singing Forest, through the diamond-strewn Kalahar Valley, and toward the golden seas of desert sand.

Twenty, fifty, a hundred miles and more.

By noon, they ventured across the border of Lumpland, between two ranges of high dunes, and headed straight south.

"I'm scared," Keeah admitted, urging her pilka up the ring of tall dunes that protected the Lumpy capital. "The sandstorm I saw was terrible. I'm afraid of what we'll find — oh!"

Coming over the last rise, the five friends stopped. The sandstorm Keeah had seen was gone. But in its place was something even worse.

The royal village was a shambles. The bustling home of the purple Lumpies was utterly lifeless. Its houses were wrecked. Its dunes were trampled by thousands of hoof prints. The domed palace of Khan, the king, which was no more than a small house to begin with, was nearly destroyed. Two of its five walls were crumbled to dust.

Keeah sniffled and wiped away a tear. "Oh, Lumpies!"

Max jumped to the ground and examined the prints in the sand. "Hundreds of hooves galloped in a circle around the village, probably causing the sandstorm you saw earlier. And I know what kind of hooves they were. Sand pony hooves! My friends, there is only one tribe that uses sand ponies for things like this. This is the dirty work of . . . the Snitchers!"

"The Snitchers?" gasped Julie.

"The Rat-faced Snitchers?" asked Eric, frowning.

"Of Zoop!" added Neal. "Man, such a cool name for such an uncool people."

The children had met the Snitchers before. On a journey into the past, they had freed young Galen from a band of the odd little creatures. The Rat-faced Snitchers of Zoop were highwaymen who rode the

dunes on little ponies, stealing from inno-
cent people.

"But this is new," said Keeah, sliding
from her saddle to the ground in front of
Khan's broken house. "The Snitchers have
never attacked a whole village before. I
wonder if someone put them up to this."

Eric wondered the same thing. His
first thought was that Emperor Ko, leader
of the beasts of the Dark Lands, was behind
it. "Ko is usually behind most evil things,"
he said.

"But why would he use Snitchers?"
asked Julie. "They're not the sharpest tools
in the shed, if you know what I mean."

"And what does he want with the
Lumpies?" asked Neal. "They're just regu-
lar people — I mean, pillows."

Eric put his hand into the pouch on his
belt and took out the Ruby Orb. It flickered
once in his hand, and a scene appeared

from the *Dragonfly*'s cockpit. The plane was moving over a snow-covered valley, beginning to descend toward the center of the northern storm. Before long, the storm obscured everything, just as it had in his dream, though the snow was still white.

"I'll fly up to Khan's roof to see what I can see," said Julie.

"Me, too," said Neal. He untied the end of his turban and wound it under his chin like a helmet strap. He smiled. "Race you?"

"You're on!" Julie cried.

The two friends soared up to the top of the brown, sandy-colored dome of Khan's little palace. As they scanned in every direction, the others fanned out on the ground to look for any signs of life.

The gently winding streets were rutted and uneven. The ground had been torn up by hundreds of sand ponies. The children peeked inside every house nearby, but found no one.

All at once, Julie called down. "Guys, you can't see it from down there, but there are hoof prints and boot prints and sticks strewn around the foot of the great dune."

"It looks like the Snitchers and Lumpies had a battle right there," added Neal.

The children rushed to the base of the high dune at the eastern edge of the village. Its sands shone gold in the midday sun.

"Could something be hidden inside the dune, or under it?" asked Eric. "Something that Khan and his people fought to protect?"

"What are we waiting for?" said Keeah. "Come on, everyone. Let's dig!"

They all started shoveling handfuls of sand away from the pile. But no sooner was sand removed from the dune than it drifted right back. Every handful of sand the kids took away returned to the dune in a flash.

"This is impossible!" said Julie. "We're getting nowhere —"

"Wait," said Max. "Keeah, could this be . . . *living sand*?"

The princess's eyes went wide. "Of course! Galen told me the sand of Pethkaloo has magical properties. It's used to keep robbers from finding what's buried beneath it."

"Then how are we going to find anything ourselves?" asked Neal.

Keeah smiled. "Galen told me the magic words to use, too. Give me some space, people."

Everyone moved several paces away. Keeah swung her arms wide and spun around on one foot, whispering a strange chant.

A terrific *whoosh*ing sound came from the dune. Sands flew up, then rained back down like a glittering golden shower. Next, a giant column of sand exploded out of the ground. Then another, and another. In all, four towers burst up in a wide square. In its center, thrusting from the depths of the dune, came a towering pyramid. Higher and higher it grew until it loomed over the tiny village. Running up the side was a narrow set of stairs that ended in an open doorway.

"That's one big sand castle!" said Neal.

"And —" crowed a voice, "— it's ours!"

The surrounding dunes were suddenly alive with the jingling of bells and the snorting of animals.

"Sand ponies!" snarled Max. "They're all around us!"

"It's the Snitchers!" said Julie.

"The Rat-faced Snitchers," said Keeah.

"Of Zoop!" added Neal.

"At your service!" shouted the same voice. "I mean, no. *Not* at your service. Not at all!"

Keeah's fingers sparked. Eric's did, too. They would have used their powers against the bandits, except for one thing. Tied to each Snitcher saddle like a protective shield was a captured Lumpy!

"You're horrible!" cried Julie. "How could you tie up our friends?"

"With chains," snarled the robber.

A single sand pony stepped forward. On it rode a Snitcher with grizzled whiskers. He wore a red tunic and billowy green pants, with a long yellow scarf tied on his head like a hat. Khan himself was bound to his saddle.

"I am Captain Plundit!" the bandit said, twisting his whiskers. "And the treasure in that castle is ours!"

"Thief! Robber! What have you done with my father?" demanded Keeah. "Where is Zello, King of Droon?"

"He's right over there!" said Captain Plundit. He pointed to a nearby dune, where King Zello was crouched on his knees, bound by chains from head to toe.

"I'm all right," called Zello. "He tricked me. He tricked us all!"

"Of course I did!" Captain Plundit squeaked. "But never mind that. Thanks to your magic charm, Princess, the treasure has finally been revealed to us. And we shall have it."

"What *is* the treasure?" asked Eric.

"A . . . thing," said the captain, vaguely.

"What kind of thing?" asked Julie.

Plundit frowned. "The kind of thing that is a treasure, that's what!"

"You don't even know what it is, do you?" asked Keeah.

"Maybe," Plundit mumbled.

"I didn't think so," Keeah said. "Who are you working for? Is it Emperor Ko? What did he send you to steal from the poor Lumpies?"

"Never you mind!" said a second Snitcher, twirling a club over his head. "Let's attack!"

With that, the bandits all twirled clubs over their heads.

"Wait!" called Captain Plundit. "Before we attack, we always have a song from the Snitcher troubadour. Corporal Smeed, call the troubadour!"

"Troubadour!" called the club-wielding Snitcher. "Come forth. You are requested!"

A nervous little bandit with a big stringed instrument staggered forward among the band of thieves. He coughed, and adjusted the strap holding an instrument that looked like a cross between a banjo and a ukulele.

Captain Plundit stood up on his pilka's saddle. He folded his arms and glared at the children below. Even standing full height on the back of a pilka, the Snitcher leader was still no taller than an elf.

"Sing!" Captain Plundit commanded.

The bandits quieted, and the song began.

Captain Plundit is his name
And snitching treasures is his game.
It also is his greatest fame,
And that's the reason why we came!

"Hmmm," said Plundit. "I *like* it!"

"It's also pretty lame," said Neal, "to have your rhymes all sound the same."

The troubadour blinked. "Wow. Maybe *you* should be the Snitcher troubadour —"

"Enough!" said Plundit. He twisted his whiskers again. He dug his tiny feet into his tiny stirrups. "Ready, my fellows?"

"Ready!" the Snitchers hooted.

"Let's attack!"

The little ponies whinnied, sand flew, clubs whizzed, and the battle of the dunes began!

The Big Attack

"Hi-yaaa-hee-ooo!" yelled the rat-faced robbers. They galloped down the dunes.

Keeah pulled her friends back toward the pyramid. "I don't know what this building is all about," she said. "But if the Snitchers want to get inside, it's our job to keep them out!"

"Defense!" cried Neal, tightening his turban.

"Pilkas!" shouted Max. "Surround the treasure house!"

The shaggy-furred beasts did as he said. There were so many attackers, however, that the little band was soon overwhelmed. And with the Lumpies tied to the robbers' saddles, neither Keeah nor Eric could fire a single blast for fear of harming their friends.

To make matters worse, the Snitchers were being egged on by their troubadour, who kept singing one victory song after another.

We will take,
You will quake!

and

You won't grin
When we win!

With each new rhyme, the little troops advanced closer to the pyramid.

"We're way outnumbered," said Julie.

"Cover me, boys — I'm going into the treasure house!" yelled Plundit, and he slid Khan off his saddle and charged the pyramid.

The robber leader was small, but he proved to be a very good pony rider. He nudged the animal's flanks, and it bounded up the pyramid, three steps at a time. Before anyone could stop him, Plundit disappeared into the dark opening, laughing at the top of his lungs.

"Someone follow him!" Keeah shouted, busy helping Max and Julie try to stop any more Snitchers from scaling the steps.

"Neal, we can do this!" said Eric.

As Keeah, Julie, and Max kicked sand at the robbers and blocked their way to the castle, Neal and Eric hustled up the steps toward the pyramid's summit. Without a pause, they dived together through the opening.

The moment they stepped inside, all the sounds of the battle outside — the hollering, the whinnying ponies, the calls of their friends, the squeals of the Lumpies — stopped.

"This place really is magical," Neal whispered.

"Let's hope it works for us," said Eric. "Come on. We have to keep Sergeant Plundit from running off with the treasure —"

"That's *Captain* Plundit to you!" came a yell from up ahead.

"Touchy, isn't he?" said Neal, hurrying toward the sound of the voice, with Eric on his heels.

The passages inside the pyramid were narrow and dark. They zigzagged steeply downward, then continued as if they wound deep under the ground.

Eric ran his finger along the wall. Sand poured to the floor from where he touched. "It really is one giant sand castle. I can't risk shooting sparks around in here —"

Neal paused. "Look at that."

Plundit's sand pony stood in the passage ahead, stamping lazily on the floor.

Its rider was nowhere in sight.

"He's gone ahead on foot," said Eric, following the marks on the floor to where the ceiling of the passage lowered. "And then on his hands and knees."

"I don't like tight spaces," said Neal.

"That makes two of us. Come on."

The two friends crawled into the narrow passage after the robber. The tunnel soon opened out into a room as large as a gymnasium, whose walls seemed to go on forever.

Captain Plundit was already halfway down a long set of stairs. In the center of the otherwise empty floor below sat a small box the size of a shoe box. It appeared to be made of wood, but was crisscrossed in heavy chains.

"It's here! I have it!" crowed the Snitcher. He jumped off the stairs and ran to the chest.

Eric and Neal bounded after him.

"You leave that alone!" yelled Eric.

"Try and stop me!" snarled Plundit.

"That's exactly what we —" Neal began.

But the instant Plundit snatched the chest up from the floor, the walls around them wobbled sharply. Sand rained down from the ceiling. The walls began to crack. The floor sank beneath their feet.

"Uh-oh," said Neal. "Booby trap . . ."

"Worse — magical booby trap!" cried Eric.

Before either boy could make a move, Plundit flung a handful of sand at them and darted past with the chest, racing up the stairs to his pony.

"Eric, Neal, get out of there!" Keeah cried from the pyramid's opening. "The castle is crumbling!"

"Run!" cried Neal. He grabbed Eric's hand and pulled him up the steps as fast as he could. They hurried back through the passages, even as the walls collapsed one by one behind them.

Keeah yanked both boys out of the entrance and down the stairs, seconds before the whole pyramid collapsed back into the ground.

Laughing wildly, Captain Plundit galloped past Neal, Julie, and Max and joined his men. Holding the chest high, he yelled, "Let's take the treasure to Zoop and see what it is!"

"We'll follow you," said Keeah. "And we'll get that treasure back."

"I'm so scared!" snarled Plundit. "Besides, you'll never find Zoop. It's completely hidden —"

"In the black mountain!" said Smeed, pointing to the distant east.

Plundit turned to him. "Good work, bigmouth! You told them where Zoop is. Now they'll come after us."

"But they'll never find it," said Smeed. "I didn't mention the twin valleys, did I?"

Plundit thought for a moment. "No. But what about the rocks that look like faces? Did you say anything about them?"

"Not a word," said Smeed. "Or the mountain pass known as the Pretzel, either. Only if they follow that will they actually find Zoop. They haven't got a chance!"

Keeah stared at them. "We're right here, you know. We can hear every word you're saying."

"Oh!" growled Plundit. "Forget everything we said! To Zoop, Snitchers! Go!"

At the leader's command, the robbers untied the Lumpies and pushed them all from their saddles. Then the entire band galloped around and around the village on the sand ponies. They moved so quickly that a second sandstorm grew up, acting as a wall between them and the children.

"Those ponies are fast!" exclaimed Neal.

A moment later, they heard the sound of hooves retreating across the desert. When the sandstorm died away, Keeah raced across the dunes to her father.

"Daddy!" she said. She blasted away his bonds, and he jumped to his feet.

"I feel so silly," said the king. "I found a way through the sandstorm and into the Lumpy village, but the whole force of the Snitchers was on me in a moment. They cast me in chains before I could wield my club!"

Khan hustled over as quickly as he could. He patted the king's arm. "We battled the robbers, too, but their numbers were too great. Now they have the secret treasure!"

"What exactly is the treasure?" asked Eric.

Khan shook his head. "We don't know. My ancestors vowed to protect it from evil hands, and they did. Until today."

Zello scanned the deserts to the east. "We may not have seen Ko today, but this theft reeks of him. Khan, I will stay and help rebuild your village. Maybe we'll find a clue about this treasure. Keeah, you all must find Zoop and try to keep the trea-sure from Emperor Ko!"

Keeah hugged her father. "We'll do it."

Max saluted. "Aye-aye, my king!" He leaped back onto his pilka and called to the others. "Hi-ya! To the distant caves —"

"Of Zoop!" added Neal.

As quickly as they could, the five friends raced across the dunes toward the hideout of the dastardly Rat-faced Snitchers!

Five

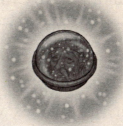

Storm of Snow, Storm of Sand

Mile after mile vanished under the pilkas' thunderous hooves, but as little as the sand ponies were, they were fast. Before long, the robbers had vanished from sight.

Keeah slowed her pilka. "The desert ponies don't get as tired in the heat as our northern pilkas do," she said. "We have to find water — and shade. The pilkas must rest if we have any hope of finding Zoop."

"Excuse me!" coughed a voice behind Eric.

"Eric, your pouch is talking," said Neal.

"And it's talking in my master's voice," said Max. "It is the Ruby Orb!"

Eric flipped open his pouch. The red sphere of Doobesh popped out and hovered in the air, its insides whirling with snow. Galen's face appeared through the flakes. The children quickly told him what they had found.

"But we're falling behind," said Julie. "And we're running out of time."

"I see," said Galen, seeming to stare at Neal's head. "Yes, I see. In fact, I *see* only one thing . . . and it looks like a big blueberry!"

"That's Neal's turban," said Julie.

"Ah, yes," said Galen. "His *genie* turban. The turban whose magical cloth has been known to turn into water. Water, as in a swiftly moving river. Neal, use your head —"

The boy gasped. "A river! Right! I can make a river from my hat! A river to follow the Snitchers on! My good old genie turban!"

"My work here is done," said Galen, and the Orb flickered out.

Neal whipped the giant blue bundle of fabric off his head. Standing on the back of his pilka, he held one end of the cloth tightly and hurled the rest toward where the robbers had disappeared.

Phewwwww! The cloth unrolled and fluttered down onto the sand. But when it did, it was no longer a cloth. It was a bubbling blue river that surged miles and miles across the deserts toward eastern Droon.

"*Voilà!*" said Julie. "Instant river!"

Rushing to a nearby oasis, the friends collected branches, tree bark, and palm leaves.

Using his spider silk like glue, Max wove all the pieces together and secured them as tightly as he could. When he stepped back, a small round boat and five paddles sat on the bank of the flowing river.

"A not-so-instant watercraft!" Max said.

Keeah whispered to the pilkas. They each nodded and trotted quickly back toward the Lumpy village.

One by one, the five friends stepped into the boat. Digging their palm-leaf paddles into the water, they launched the boat from the shore. It sped instantly down the river.

"Whoo-hoo!" said Neal. "What a good turban. Now we're really moving!"

Even as the boat approached the first of the landmarks the Snitchers had mentioned, Eric couldn't help but study the Ruby Orb. Snow filled the inside of the glass ball, but it was still just white snow.

Maybe they aren't far enough north yet, he thought. *Blue snow was part of the legend.*

Max peered into the Orb and sucked in air between his teeth. "They have already gone far beyond the Ice Hills of Tarabat."

Eric remembered how, on their very first adventure in Droon, Keeah had taken them to the Ice Hills. Now he really wanted to retrieve the treasure from the Snitchers, but the north called him, too. He wanted to go on every journey in Droon, to do everything he possibly could.

As they kept paddling in the direction the Snitchers had gone, the river began to drop.

"The twin valleys," said Keeah. "Hold on!"

The river suddenly cascaded wildly down a slope and into a valley, then into a second valley identical to the first.

The boat thudded at the bottom of the drop, then whirled around and around until the kids managed to steady it. As they rounded a bend in the river, they lifted their oars, staring at the twin mounds of sand flanking the river.

"Either people in this part of Droon look a lot like stones," said Max, "or we've found the rocks that look like faces."

Two squat stones stood nearby, like guards at attention. A bulge in the upper part of each stone looked like a nose with an eye on either side of it.

"Uh-oh," said Neal, peering at the faces. "The stones may not be alive, but those snakes are!"

Everyone looked to see long black snakes crawling out of the eyes and ears of the two head-shaped rocks. The snakes snarled and bared triple rows of long green teeth.

"Sand stingers!" said Keeah.

"I knew it!" yelped Max. "The stingers are Ko's deadly pets. The emperor truly is behind this —"

"Paddle for your lives!" said Keeah. "Go!"

But no matter how quickly the children dug their paddles into the water, they couldn't escape the snakes. Dozens slithered down the bank and splashed into the water, hissing and snarling with tongues that flashed like whips.

"Blast them, Keeah," said Eric. "Together!"

The two children's fingers sparked and they sent bolt after searing bolt onto the attackers.

Blam! Ka-blam!

The air lit up with explosions. The two wizards managed to keep the snakes at bay for a while, but more and more crawled down the banks and into the river. All of a sudden, a trio of stingers leaped up onto the boat and coiled around Max's legs.

"No, no! I'm caught. Help!" he cried.

It was over in a moment. The snakes dragged Max off the boat. He splashed into the water, then flailed wildly as the stingers dragged him up onto land.

"Help me!" he cried.

But there was nothing that Eric and his friends could do. They couldn't risk hurting their friend by fighting back! Holding Max tightly, the snakes slithered swiftly across the sands toward the black mountain.

"After him —" said Julie, digging her paddle into the water with determination. "Hurry!"

Suddenly, the boat quivered from port to starboard, and waves heaved and splashed over the side, drenching the children. With a terrible sucking sound, the little craft was lifted clear out of the water.

"Uh-oh!" said Neal, grabbing tight to the sides of the boat. "We're going over . . ."

SPLASH! In a single move, the snakes flipped the boat over and tossed it hard into the water. It shuddered from stem to stern, broke apart, and sank straight to the bottom.

Six

Zoop, Zoop, and More Zoop!

Glub! Blub! The four friends flailed in the churning waves, desperate to stay afloat.

The river was filling with snarling snakes.

Eric gulped air and went down. Taking aim, he blasted under the water, hurtling a slew of snakes back up onto the river-bank. Then he did the same on his other side.

Take my hand! Keeah called to him silently. Eric reached out to her and rose to the surface.

Neal's head was visible, but he was splashing around wildly. "If only I had my turban, I could get us out of here!" he said.

"Your turban?" said Julie, gasping for air. "We're *drowning* in your turban —"

Neal blinked. "Oh, wow, I totally forgot!" Diving deep, he reached out with both hands as if to grab the water tightly. Then he pulled.

Sloooorp!

The river vanished beneath the friends in a flash. They found themselves sitting on dry sand amid a coil of silky blue cloth.

With two more quick blasts, Eric and Keeah chased the remaining snakes back over the sand to the twin stone heads.

Then their eyes fell upon what lay in the distance.

"Well, take a look at that," said Eric, his mouth gaping open.

A range of brown mountains stood not far away. Rising gloomily behind it was a single black peak, its top jagged and jutting high over the sands.

Eric recognized it as a volcano. Its charred summit rose high over the lower mountains. Near its peak was the dark opening of a cave. There, flames flickered like a jewel on a necklace.

"I think we found Zoop," said Neal, giving a low whistle. "People, the snakes took Max to Zoop. The Snitchers are in Zoop. The treasure is in Zoop. I think we'd better get to Zoop."

"You like saying Zoop, don't you?" asked Julie.

"I *do* like saying Zoop!" said Neal. "But I'll get over it. As soon as we save Max."

"Then let's do it," said Keeah.

Pulling themselves together, the four friends set off once more, this time on foot.

The friends journeyed across miles of desert. They were tired and hungry. The afternoon came and went. But they didn't slow down. They had to rescue Max!

Finally, as day edged into night, they came to the foot of the ash-covered mountain. Cliffs rose straight up from the ground to a gnarled summit.

The volcano seemed alive with fires flaring in its many smaller caves and its large, central opening near the top. Torches glowed up and down the rocks, signaling that dozens of bandits patrolled the mountainside.

Thumpety-thump!

The sound of hooves rapidly approached. The children darted into hiding and watched as hundreds of

whiskered bandits tore over the dunes and up into a twisting mountain pass they knew was called the Pretzel.

"We're even more outnumbered than before," said Julie. "How many Snitchers are coming together in this place?"

"Too many to guard one small treasure, no matter how priceless," said Keeah. "Something big is going on here. We could use some help. Maybe we should contact Galen. Eric, let's use the Orb."

Eric took the Ruby Orb from the wizard's pouch and held it in his hand. The sphere felt lifeless, heavy. Nothing showed in its center. "I don't know. Maybe they're in the dark?"

Julie leaned in. "Galen? Can you hear us?"

There was no image, no movement in the Orb, no change at all.

"Maybe they got separated from the Orb," said Neal. "Maybe the Sapphire Star is lost."

Keeah eyed the unending stream of bandits working their way to the summit of the volcano. "Then we'll have to go up alone."

"There's one way to get Galen," said Julie. "It's a long way, but if I fly north, maybe I can see him. I'll be back before you miss me."

"Are you sure?" asked Neal. "I mean, not about missing you, but the north is one giant storm. And you'd be all alone —"

Julie gave him a smile. "Don't worry, I'll be fine."

Neal frowned. "Just be careful."

"I will." Glancing around to make sure that no Snitchers spied her, Julie leaped up into the air. As if caught by a gust of sudden wind, she soared up into the air like a bird. Her friends watched her circle the mountain. Night was falling swiftly, and they soon lost sight of her.

"First we climb. Then we wait," said Keeah.

The three friends climbed through a series of mazelike passes as quickly as they could. They approached the Snitcher camp in time to see several bandits hustle Max into the large cave near the summit.

"He looks okay," said Eric. "He's Max, after all. But if Julie doesn't come back soon, we might have to go in ourselves —"

Crunch! The children fell silent. They saw a head moving among the rocks below them.

"A spy!" said Neal. "Nobody move."

They watched the figure climb one rock after another until he was directly below them.

A troop of Snitchers raced up through the pass. Instead of hailing them, however, the figure jumped behind a rock and went still.

"He's hiding from the bandits," whispered Keeah. "Maybe he's a friend. . . ."

The Snitchers passed, trailing a peculiar smell behind them.

"Hold on a minute!" whispered Neal. He sniffed from left to right, and back again. "Guys, I smell cheese!"

"Neal," said Eric. "This is not the time —" Then he stopped. "Wait. I smell cheese, too."

Then they all smelled it.

As the figure climbed again, it passed through a shaft of moonlight, and the children realized that it was an Orkin.

These were creatures who were once angry Ninn warriors, but who had reverted to their original state — plump, cheese-loving, mild-mannered, blue-faced Orkins!

Not only that, but this was an Orkin they knew.

"Djambo!" whispered Eric, jumping down to him. "Djambo! It's us!"

The blue-faced friend blinked when he saw Eric and the others, then grinned from ear to ear. "My friends! It's been forever!"

"It *has* been forever," Keeah agreed. "But what are you doing here?"

"In Zoop?" added Neal.

Djambo sighed as he glanced toward the Snitcher camp. "I'm searching for something. A treasure has been stolen from its hiding place."

The children shared a look.

"Is it in a small wooden box?" asked Keeah.

Djambo blinked. "It is!"

"We're looking for it, too," said Eric. "We were there when the Snitchers stole it from a magic sand castle. They also stole Max!"

Djambo clucked his tongue. "Bad, bad bandits," he muttered.

"What is the treasure, exactly?" asked Keeah.

"A gift from above," said the Orkin. "A very special object. A blue snowflake."

Eric's heart skipped a beat. "A blue snowflake? I dreamed of blue snowflakes!"

Djambo smiled at Eric. "Then you are blessed with great vision, my boy. For while we know *what* the treasure is, only one person has ever seen it. We Orkins vowed to protect it from the moment it was found a hundred years ago — *hush!*"

Brum! Brumma-brum! The bandits marched loudly to the sound of the troubadour's song.

"Please tell us what you know," said Keeah, once they realized they wouldn't be overheard.

As the fire crackled in the caves above, Djambo began. "It started exactly one hundred years ago, with an army of Ninns on a mission for Lord Sparr in the far north. From nowhere comes thunder and lightning. The earth shakes. The sky shakes. The stars move! A tremendous storm falls on the army. One of the Ninns sees a serpent — a *blue* serpent — falling through the sky. Then, there is a crash as it strikes the frozen wastes."

"That's where Galen is now," said Keeah.

The Orkin nodded somberly. "No soul remains from that time. What *does* remain is a single scale from the serpent. It is in the shape of a blue snowflake. It fell from the sky. The moment the Ninn caught it, he instantly became an Orkin! He was my great-uncle. He was known as Mudji, 'the one who changed.' He is why it's called the Orkin treasure."

"Incredible," said Keeah quietly. "But how did it get to Lumpland?"

"Ahh," said Djambo. "Knowing that the snowflake was magic, and fearing that Sparr would want it for his own uses, Mudji escaped. He vowed to hide it where it could not be found. Armed with a special key and an unbreakable box, he buried it in Lumpland, under magic sand that a peddler had sold him —"

"The living sand of Pethkaloo," said Keeah. "We saw that magical sand castle."

Djambo nodded. "And it was hidden. Evil hands did not possess the treasure, until today. I fought the Snitchers once. I will do it again."

Keeah scanned the camp above them. "The question is . . . why do the Snitchers want the treasure?"

Djambo frowned. "I know only one thing. I must steal it back at whatever cost —"

"The cost is going to be high, with just four of us against hundreds," said Neal.

Eric removed the Ruby Orb from its pouch again. Now it was whirling with wind and waves of snow. He hoped Julie would find Galen soon. He was sure their journey in the desert and Galen's in the far north were connected. And both journeys were becoming far more serious than Eric had imagined.

"I think I know how to get us into their camp," said Eric.

"And back out again?" asked Neal.

Eric smiled. "If we're lucky." He turned to Djambo. "You said you've tangled with the Snitchers before. What if you became their prisoner?"

Djambo blinked. "I'm sure they'd like that very much, but I wouldn't like it at all."

"Even if *we* capture you?" asked Eric. "Disguised as beasts?"

The Orkin frowned at first, then he began to smile. "Oh, I see! By capturing me, we get into their camp. Very clever!"

"I know a beast spell," said Keeah. "It only lasts half an hour. But it may be our one chance to find Max and get that treasure."

"Please don't turn me into a fish again," said Neal. "Sparr once changed me into a fish that shouted really loudly. I didn't like it one bit."

Keeah smiled. "I'll try my best to avoid it."

Djambo laughed. "Are we ready, then?"

Keeah closed her eyes, spoke a long string of words, then waved her arms over herself, Eric, and Neal. At once, they began to change.

Eric tried to stand, but slumped over on all fours. He realized that he was covered in thick green fur, and had eyes in both the front and back of his head. He remembered he had been this shape before!

Keeah sprouted feathers and long, graceful wings, with an ungainly pair of antlers growing from her forehead. She struggled to keep her head from falling forward.

Neal was not as lucky. He shrank to the size of a dog, but remained upright, was covered with scales, and had a tail and three feet.

"OH, NO!" he shouted. "NOT THE FISH AGAIN! KEEAH, YOU PROMISED!"

"Sorry, Neal," she said. "I said I'd try."

"Think of it this way," said Eric. "Your shouting might scare the Snitchers."

"WHY NOT?" Neal shouted. "IT SURE SCARES ME!"

Holding Djambo gently by the arms, the three children disguised as beasts marched straight into the Snitcher camp.

"MAKE WAY! MAKE WAY!" Neal yelled. "WE HAVE A PRISONER!"

Seven

Hoola-moola!

The Snitcher guards jumped when they saw beasts entering their camp and shouting at the top of their lungs.

"OUT OF THE WAY, BANDITS! WE FOUND US AN ORKIN SPY!"

"An Orkin!" cried the robber named Corporal Smeed. He scurried over to them with a squad of Snitchers. "And beasts! Beasts who have come into our humble camp! Did the great Ko send you?"

The children looked at one another.

"SURE, HE SENT US!" Neal shouted. "WE'RE HIS SPECIAL FRIENDS. YOU'D BETTER DO WHAT WE SAY!"

The Snitchers shrank back. Corporal Smeed quaked in his boots. "Please don't hurt us!"

"Then don't make us mad!" Eric growled in a voice as deep as he could make it.

"Please come," said Smeed. "Captain Plundit will want to see you immediately."

Keeah and Eric held Djambo loosely as the friends tramped noisily through the camp.

They found Plundit standing on a small stool amid a circle of mesmerized robbers. He wore a pair of wide-barreled pistols in his belt. He held the treasure box high while inventing the story of how he'd gotten it.

"One thousand Lumpies with cutlasses! Hundreds of spark-shooting wizards! Hah! I vanquished them all!" he declared.

"Yay!" cheered the Snitchers.

"I sank a navy, too —" he started.

But then his eyes went wide when he saw beasts in his camp. "Yikes!" he cried, jumping down from his stool "How . . . how . . . *wonderful* that you have joined us today. With a prisoner! This Orkin will tell me exactly what I need to know. Bring him forward, if you please."

Djambo whispered to the children. "I have a plan. One of you stay with me while the others search for Max. I'll try to trick Plundit into letting go of the treasure, even briefly."

"You got it," whispered Eric. "Neal, I volunteer you. And be loud. You're a beast."

"HOW CAN I FORGET?" Neal shouted.

He pretended to push Djambo, while Keeah and Eric backed away, step by step.

"So," said Plundit, his grin revealing several missing teeth. "I want to unlock this treasure box! Tell me, or I will force you to!"

"YEAH, FORCE YOU!" shouted Neal.

Djambo closed his eyes. "The . . . oh, I cannot lie! The box is under a magic spell. Unless the box is opened the right way, it will explode into a million pieces!"

"Ahhh!" Plundit set the box on the ground and jumped away from it. "What kind of treasure is that? Ko can open it himself when he comes for it —"

When he comes? thought Eric. *So we were right. Ko is definitely behind the theft.*

But why?

Why does he want the blue snow-flake?

Plundit pushed his whiskery face into Djambo's great blue one and scowled. "Wait a second! *You* must know the spell. You can open it, can't you? Of course you can! It's an Orkin treasure. You're an Orkin. I demand that you open it!"

"He demands it!" snarled Smeed.

"WE ALL DEMAND IT!" said Neal.

Djambo tried to look frightened. "I know the spell, but everyone must help."

Djambo turned to wink at Neal, then turned back. "If it works, the box should begin to float off the ground. Snitchers, repeat after me: '*Hoola-moola-moola-hoola*.'"

"*Hoola-moola!*" said the Snitchers. "*Moola-hoola!*"

With a discreet twist of his fingers, Neal used a genie trick to make the box turn slowly in the air.

"Now that's what I'm talking about!" snarled Plundit. "Do more of that!"

"YEAH, DO MORE!" said Neal.

Good luck, Eric spoke silently to his friend. Then he and Keeah sidled away from the campfire. Moving carefully backward, they made their way to the mouth of the giant cave and darted inside before anyone saw them.

The passages twisted and turned, dipped and rose as the two friends hastened farther and farther into the depths of the volcano.

"Max? Max!" they whispered at every corner. Hearing no answer, they hurried on.

"Eric, we don't have much time," said Keeah. "I feel my spell wearing off a little."

"Me, too," said Eric. "Besides, Plundit is a little nutty. If he suspects he's being tricked, he'll capture us all. Max, do you hear me?"

A shaft of moonlight as narrow as a flashlight beam shone into the passage ahead.

"Oh my gosh," said Keeah. "Is that the shaft of the volcano?"

Eric gulped. "I'm glad this mountain is dormant. Let's keep going."

But they couldn't keep going. The moment they crossed the light, the mountain around them trembled, and rocks — little ones at first, then larger ones — began to tumble down the shaft, carrying a cloud of ash with them.

"It's raining rocks!" said Keeah. "Move —"

All of a sudden, the shaft darkened, and a big rock dropped toward them.

A *very* big rock.

"Keeah, run back!" said Eric.

"I can't see!" she cried.

They tripped over each other and tumbled to the ground.

Just as they tried to get up, they were struck squarely on their heads by the giant stone.

THWUMPPP!

Eight

A Gift From Above

Except that it wasn't a giant stone.

It was Julie.

"Oww, my foot!"

"Oww, my face!" Eric moaned. He opened his eyes to find a pink sneaker on his forehead. "Hey," he grumbled, pushing it off.

Julie jumped to her feet. "Beasts!"

"It's us!" said Keeah.

Julie stared at her friends. "Oh, sorry. I thought I would sneak into camp the back way. When I saw the mouth of the volcano, it seemed perfect. Who knew that you two were playing explorers down here?"

"We're not playing explorers," said Keeah, dusting herself off. "We're exploring for real. Trying to find Max."

"What about Galen?" said Eric.

"And my mother?" said Keeah. "We really need them. And I mean *really*."

Julie let out a deep breath. "About that. They're sort of . . . not coming."

"Not coming!" said Eric.

She shook her head. "I saw a snowstorm as big as a hurricane north of the Tarabat Hills. Galen, Friddle, and the queen tried to push through it, but they got more and more lost. Finally, the storm drove them into a deep chasm. I tried to help, but the winds kept blowing me away. I couldn't get near them."

Eric shook his head. "It's been like this all day. We keep losing help. We'll have to find Max, steal back the treasure, and battle the Snitchers by ourselves."

Keeah took a breath. "We're on our own."

"Except that Captain Plundit and his boys aren't your biggest worry right now," said Julie. "Just before I flew into the volcano, I saw something that nobody's going to like."

Eric groaned. "Don't tell me. No, go ahead."

Julie gave him a look. "I saw —"

"No, wait. Don't say it," he said.

She frowned. "Eric —"

"Never mind. It's okay. Tell me."

"I saw two —"

Eric groaned. "I know it's going to be bad!"

Julie looked at Keeah. They both shrugged.

"All right," said Eric. "Wait . . . okay —"

"I saw two horns spouting fire!" Julie blurted out. "It's Ko! He's coming right now!"

Eric hung his head. "You see? That's exactly what I didn't want to know. I knew Ko was involved. But why? Why does he want a little snowflake? I don't know why, but he wants it —"

"Shhh!" said Keeah, tilting her head. "My beast ears must be really good, because I hear something coming." She closed her eyes.

Eric heard it, too. It was the sound of feet bounding rapidly toward them along the passages. "Get ready to fight!" Eric whispered.

All of a sudden, a shape ran by. But it wasn't a Snitcher. Or a real beast.

It had eight legs and wild orange hair.

"Max!" said Julie. "You're free!"

"I'm free!" the spider troll exclaimed, staring at Eric and Keeah in alarm.

"Max, it's us," said Keeah. "We're beasts."

He looked relieved. "I just fought off a crew of silly Snitchers," he said. "They won't go gallivanting for a while, that's for sure."

"Max," said Eric, "Galen's not coming. No one is coming to help us."

"Except for Ko," said Julie. "He's coming. But not to help us."

Max started pacing up and down the passage. "Things aren't going well, are they?"

"No," said Eric, pacing up and down the passage with him. "No, they aren't."

"On the other hand, it could be worse," said the spider troll. "I could still be a captive. There must be a way five smart friends can take back that treasure and get out of Zoop."

"Six friends," said Keeah. "Djambo is here."

Max grinned. "Our numbers grow!"

Eric stopped pacing. "I have it, I think. Max and Julie, listen. Plundit and the other Snitchers don't know you're free. I say we keep it that way. You go to the top of the shaft and get ready to surprise the baddies from above with some kind of distraction."

Max grinned. "I have a few tricks in mind."

"Meanwhile," said Keeah, "Eric and I will help Neal and Djambo get the treasure back."

Eric nodded. "That's the idea."

"It actually sounds like a plan," said Julie. "I just hope it works."

Eric smiled. "We all hope it works."

While Max climbed, and Julie flew up the shaft and out its opening at the top, Keeah and Eric quietly and carefully made their way through the passages.

"I really don't feel good about my plan," said Eric.

"It needs a lot of luck," said Keeah. "But it's the best we have. Besides, we're still in beast disguises. So as long as you watch my back and I watch yours, we should be okay."

"It's actually not your back I'm worried about," said Eric. "It's your nose. Your beak is fading and your real nose is starting to show through."

Keeah put her hand to her face. "I'll keep my head down. Let's do this fast."

But the moment they left the passage and entered the camp outside, they froze.

A great golden chariot pulled by two lion-headed beasts raced up the mountain pass and into the Snitcher camp. The lions growled three times like thunder, then went silent.

Standing in the chariot was the towering figure of Emperor Ko himself. His twin horns blazed with green fire.

"Max sure was right when he said things weren't going well, wasn't he?" said Eric.

"He's smart that way," whispered Keeah.

"Where is my treasure?" boomed Ko, his three red eyes coldly scanning the camp.

As the bandits backed away, step by step, Neal and Djambo joined Eric and Keeah, leaving Plundit standing mesmerized by the floating treasure chest.

"Plundit!" shouted Ko.

The bandit leader jumped, then squealed loudly. "Ko? Oh! All hail the emperor!"

"ALL HAIL!" Neal added.

Ko leaped from his chariot and fixed his eyes on the children. Green, foul-smelling flames spurted noisily from his horns into the night sky.

"You beasts, halt where you are!" he shouted at the children, stomping straight toward them.

"I'm going to be honest," whispered Keeah. "Not only do things not look good, they look downright bad."

Eric nodded. "You got that right."

"OH, YEAH!" said Neal.

Nine

Enemies in High Places

"Halt where you are," Ko repeated. "And come to my special chamber! We will eat and discuss old times!"

"EAT?" said Neal. "AS IN . . . FOOD?"

"Uh . . . okay," said Eric. Glancing up, he saw Max and Julie on a ridge high above them. He shook his head.

Wait. Not yet! he said silently to Julie. She nodded in agreement.

"Plundit!" Ko boomed. "Bring that Orkin and the treasure box inside with us!"

The little group went into the large cave together. Ten paces in, they entered a chamber far larger than the others, outfitted with furniture too large for the Snitchers.

Wall torches flared brightly, then dimmed, as if the flames themselves were afraid of Ko.

"My home away from home," grunted the emperor, slumping into a throne. "Ha, ha!"

While four Snitchers held Djambo, Plundit placed the treasure box in Ko's giant hands. Then he backed away until he bumped the wall and stopped.

"Arthus!" said Ko. "Come sit by me."

The children glanced at one another. No one moved.

"Arthus?" Ko repeated. He swiveled toward Eric. "Why do you not move?"

"Oh! Me!" said Eric. "Of course, me. Arrgh!" He shuffled over to Ko's side.

"Arthus, do you remember when you battled the rebel monkeys of Parnesh?" asked Ko, drawing a bone from a nearby bowl and starting to chew on it.

Eric nodded slowly, aware that the spell was starting to fade. His great green paws were shrinking in front of his eyes. "There sure were a lot of them that day," he said.

Ko narrowed his eyes at Eric. "There were only two little monkeys."

"Two? Really? That few?" said Eric. "Well, it sure seemed like a lot more." He was aware his voice was losing its growly edge.

Ko's eyes narrowed even more, especially his middle one. Finally, his lips widened to show a row of dark, fanglike teeth. "Ha, ha!"

"HA!" said Neal, sniffing a bone from the bowl and dropping it back in.

Plundit laughed nervously. "Hee-hee."

Eric was inches from Ko's face. It was the first time he'd ever been close enough to see beyond Ko's terrifying expression. What he saw when he looked into the beast's fiery eyes frightened him. He had long felt that Ko suffered defeats because he had weaknesses. But as he gazed at Ko, he saw that when the emperor failed, it was because he had relied on others. The ruler of the Dark Lands himself was both strong and extremely powerful.

More than that, there was a cleverness about him that Eric had not seen before.

"Come closer, my Arthus," said Ko, his voice softening. "I shall tell you a secret."

A secret! From Ko! Eric hoped his disguise lasted long enough to hear it. "Yes?"

"Do you know what I have just done?"

EATEN A CLOVE OF GARLIC? Neal yelled silently to his friends. ***THE GUY'S BREATH IS WAY BAD —***

Shhh! said Eric, slapping his paws on his ears. He felt his disguise fading more quickly by the moment. He had only minutes left.

"What have you done?" he asked Ko.

"This treasure, this single tiny treasure that I have obtained, is a key that unlocks one of the greatest secrets in the history of Droon!"

Eric trembled. "What . . . secret?"

"Ah . . ." whispered the emperor. He leaned even closer to Eric while his giant hands pawed the little treasure box.

"It was Gethwing who first told me about it. At first, I did not believe. Yet again and again, I studied the legends, the texts, the stars overhead, the seas below, the sun and moon and the slow

turning of time itself, and the answer was always the same!"

Staring into Eric's eyes from only inches away, Ko began to speak in an ancient tongue that Eric had never heard before. It was no more than grunts and clicks and snarls. Yet, Eric understood every word.

"Once you see this tiny treasure, you will wonder why I have sought it," Ko said. "You will wonder why I have come to Zoop myself to take possession of it."

"Yes," said Eric.

"It is because," said Ko, "this tiny treasure will do no less than unite all the sons of Zara in a single place and time. A place and time when they are most vulnerable. And one of them . . . listen here . . . one of them . . . will fall. . . ."

Eric's heart thundered inside him. *Zara's sons? All her sons? Galen, who was in the far north? Sparr, who was who-knows-where? And Urik, the eldest brother, who was lost in time?*

Fearful his disguise would fade right then and there, Eric quickly spoke in the same language of clicks and grunts. "So, by *fall*, do you mean . . . sort of . . . trip and hurt himself?"

Ko grinned cruelly and shook his head. "No, no, my old friend, I mean . . . *die*."

The cave was silent.

Eric's ears buzzed. He felt faint. Reaching secretly for the orb in his pouch, he clutched it tightly. It vibrated in his fingers.

Galen . . . Galen . . . he spoke. ***Did you hear that? Did you? Gethwing told Ko the meaning of the treasure. The sons of Zara will unite. One will . . . one will . . . just be careful. Be more careful than you've ever been before!***

"If he had lived," Ko went on with normal words, "Gethwing would have tried to steal the treasure. I knew he longed to take my place. But Gethwing is gone, vanished in the Underworld. And I have this small treasure that means so much!"

Eric felt his anger flare up. Rage rose in him and would not let him just sit there.

"Arthus!" said Keeah, staring at his feet. "Time to go!"

"YEAH!" said Neal. "TIME . . . TIME . . ."

But Eric couldn't go. Never had Ko been so close to him, and so vulnerable. He could make a move now. He could do it.

He stood up. "Ko!" he shouted.

But it was a tiny, frail shout. It was the shout of a boy, not a beast. In the same moment, his disguise evaporated completely, and he was Eric Hinkle once more.

Keeah's spell faded. Neal's did, too.

"Uh-oh," said Neal.

"Spies! Children —" Ko cried out.

Ko tried to leap from his chair, but as if their minds were one, Keeah and Eric blasted the emperor's throne into a hundred pieces, and Ko tumbled to the floor of the cave. In the confusion, Neal grabbed the treasure box.

"Snitchers! Capture them! Destroy them!" Ko shouted at the top of his lungs.

"Let's get out of here!" screamed Keeah. She grabbed Djambo and scrambled out of the cave to the camp outside.

"Uh-oh!" Neal cried. "Uh-oh, uh-oh! And I know we're saying that a lot today!"

"Here's something else we're saying a lot today," shouted Eric. "RUN!"

Ten

Into the Blue

Emperor Ko bounded out of the cave, his horns spouting flames high over his head. "Retrieve the treasure!" he bellowed.

"Not likely!" said Neal. Cradling the treasure box, he slapped his turban back on and leaped high over the campfire to a distant ridge.

At the same time, Keeah and Eric spun on their heels and leveled a double blast at Ko.

Blam-ka-blam! The ground at the emperor's feet exploded into rocks and ash, hurtling him flat on his back. Before he could get up, Max dropped a thick mesh of spider silk from the ridge above, and Julie flew down and twisted it around Ko so tightly that he could barely move.

"Now that's more like it!" said Keeah.

Djambo barreled into the stunned Snitcher leaders in a single move, tackling both Plundit and Smeed. This sent the other bandits squealing and running in circles.

"Cowards!" yelled Ko, struggling to escape from his bonds.

All of a sudden, there was an explosion in the camp, then another and another. Searing bolts of light flew about the rocks.

"Halt!" came a tremendous shout. "Stop where you are!"

In a flash, everyone stopped moving.

Campfires flickered out one by one, until only a single flame blazed. It cast a giant shadow of four jagged wings and a horned head against the mountain wall.

The emperor went still. "Gethwing? The moon dragon? Is it you? But . . . you died in the Underworld!"

"How dare you?" hissed the raspy voice. "You knew nothing of this treasure before I told you! Be gone now! Leave this place!"

With a blinding bolt of light, the moon dragon threw Ko — still bound in chains of spider silk — into the cliff face, stunning him.

A second bolt of light hoisted the emperor into the air and dropped him roughly into his golden chariot.

"Gethwing!" Ko shouted. "You traitor! The prophecy will come true without me — and without you! I *shall* triumph!"

A final blast of light — *ka-boom!* — snapped at the twin lions. They charged out of the camp, twisting down the mountain pass and skidding all the way to the Dark Lands.

Emperor Ko was gone.

The moon dragon remained.

"And now Snitchers . . . I will deal with you," growled the voice.

Captain Plundit squeaked, "Oh!"

For a short moment, possessing the treasure of the Orkins had made the Snitcher Captain bold. But faced with real power, he cowered and quaked.

"Please, no!" he cried. "Don't deal with the Captain of the Snitchers. It's Smeed! Smeed is really to blame —"

"Not me!" cried Smeed. "I'm as dumb as a bag of rocks! I don't know anything!"

There was no battle this time. No big attack. The Snitchers did little but run. With another stinging blast from the moon dragon, the bandits leaped to their ponies and galloped quickly down the twisted pass.

But even as they escaped, Plundit's boldness seemed to return. "After today, you can call us General Plundit and Major Smeed!" he yelped. "This was a great victory!"

"I hear a song coming!" replied Smeed.

The Snitchers vanished down the mountain to the sound of the troubadour's nervous rhyming on the word "escape."

The dragon swiveled toward the friends. "And now . . . to deal with you!"

The children were rooted to the spot.

The lone fire blazed brightly, and the dragon stepped toward them. But when it did, the shadow of its wings and horns dissolved into the uplifted cloak of a robed man.

"My friends," he said.

"Galen!" cried Max. "You are safe!"

"Safe and sound and glad to see you!" said the wizard, beaming at the children.

Keeah ran to him. "We needed you so much today!"

Still smiling, Galen looked around. "Perhaps not so much, after all."

"How did you get here?" asked Julie. "The last I saw, you were trapped in a chasm. The storm was pushing you deeper into it."

"Ah, that," said the wizard. "We *were* trapped, as you saw. Yet who should we meet in the midst of all that frozen world but a friend? He turned out to be an expert on the Great Passages themselves! He brought me here. People, say hello to . . . Mudji!"

An Orkin, blue-faced but with gray hair, stepped out from Galen's shadow.

Djambo squealed and rushed to hug the old Orkin. "After one hundred years, this is a true reunion! You are my great-uncle Mudji!"

"And you must be my grandnephew, Djambo!" said Mudji. "Together at last!"

The wizard laughed. "For all its many miles and centuries, Droon is a small world, after all."

"So, Galen," said Eric, "you heard me when I spoke to you?"

"Every word," said the wizard. "And now, my Orkin friends, please do us the honor?"

Mudji bowed. As Djambo held the treasure box, the older Orkin produced a silver key and unlocked the chest. When he lifted the lid, bright blue light shone on his face. He held the chest up, and everyone saw a snowflake as large as a silver dollar. It glistened deep blue.

Galen basked in the light of the treasure and breathed deeply. "Strange for such a tiny thing to be both full of joy and fear. If my brother wizards and I do unite, it will be a wonderful moment. And yet . . . one of us is fated to fall."

"But the prophecy could be wrong," said Eric. "It could be. There's always hope."

"This is Droon," said Keeah. "Anything can happen."

"True." Galen nodded slowly. "All things are possible. We shall see what we shall see."

The wizard smiled at Eric, but it was a sad smile. It was clear he doubted that Ko's prophecy was wrong.

"In the meantime, I predict the Snitchers will be back," said Max. "We will straighten things up for them, as they did *not* straighten up Khan's royal village.

Who knows, but one day Captain Plundit and Corporal Smeed — excuse me, General Plundit and Major Smeed — may no longer do nasty chores for Ko, but join our side in the battle to save Droon."

"We can only hope," added Djambo.

Hope. That word again. Eric had always liked the sound of it. But now, looking at the snowflake that promised so terrible a fate, he wondered if hope was their only weapon.

The little band of friends made their way down to the foot of the mountain.

"Now what?" asked Neal, looking all around. "It's usually time for us to go home right about now. But the rainbow stairs haven't come yet."

Galen smiled. "I think the answer is clear. You can't go home. The hundred-year snowstorm is in the north. The passage between our worlds is in the north. The mystery of the snowflake is in the north. So why are *we* still here?"

"You mean we're all going?" asked Eric.

"As quickly as we can!" said Galen.

At that moment, they heard the sputtering of an engine. It was the *Dragonfly*, soaring through the night sky toward them. As it came in for a landing, Eric felt his heart thump to the rhythm of the plane's engine.

All day, he had wanted to go north. All day, he had wondered why he should dream about one thing and do another. Now the answer was plain. The two journeys were really different parts of the same one. As he looked north, he knew he would soon be in the land of blue snow.

The plane bumped to a stop at the foot of the volcano. Together, the friends piled in next to Friddle and Relna, in whose hand glowed the Sapphire Star.

"You know," said Neal, "ever since I

heard that troubadour, I've been thinking we should have songs, too."

Julie shook her head. "Neal, don't —"

"Okay, I will!" he said with a laugh. Taking a deep breath, he raised his voice in song.

Let's fly into the northern snows.
We may meet friends, we may meet
* foes,*
But one thing's sure, this genie knows,
Our journey goes and goes and goes!

With that, the four-winged plane lifted from the ground, soared high over Zoop, and motored as swift as an arrow toward the ice fields of the frozen north.